Fiona —
the Lighthouse
Firefly

Judi Getch Brodman

Illustrated by Mary Licata

Judi Getch Brodman

ISBN-10: 1518721621
ISBN-13: 978-1518721625

DEDICATION

This book is dedicated to the memory of my sister, Patti Getch, who died

on May 3, 2015. It was her dream to write a story about Fiona, the

firefly. We spoke of her story ideas in the last few weeks of her life. She

knew that I would try to bring her Fiona to life.

I hope that Patti feels her dream has been fulfilled.

CONTENTS

ACKNOWLEDGMENTS

This book wouldn't have been possible without my husband Steve's love and support. He encouraged me to start it, finish it and publish it – for myself and for my sister Patti.. I love you dearly.

Fiona and Lizbeth wouldn't visually exist without the tremendous talent of my dear friend, Mary Licata, who lovingly created each illustration from my words. I can't begin to tell you how much you mean to me.

My dear sister Linda Dawson who took the time out of her own writing to read and make Fiona better, thank you and I love you.

And finally, to my friend, original writing group "fearless" leader, and writer extraordinaire, Marlene Roberts Banet, who took the time to read and provide encouraging feedback – I thank you!

1 LIZBETH

Lizbeth Bailey lives in Windy Harbor, Maine, a tiny fishing village on a finger of land that reaches out into the Atlantic Ocean. Her house, a rose covered weather worn Cape, sits outside the town on the eastern most point of the peninsula. What's most striking about her house is its view of both the lighthouse and the vast Atlantic Ocean.

Up the dirt road that leads to town stands a little wooden three room school house where Lizbeth goes to school – she's in Mrs. Riley's class. Most days, she arrives before the bell rings. When she doesn't, Mrs. Riley sends her home with a note.

Today, Lizbeth skips along the sandy lane swinging her book bag. A shadow dances across her path. Lizbeth looks up and waves to the bird circling above.

"Sally, what do you have?" Lizbeth calls, sure that Sally the seagull has something in her curled beak.

Sally ignores Lizbeth. Then, a clam shell drops. It twists and turns like a winged maple tree seed till it hits the dirt with a puff. The clam remains closed. Sally lands, squawks, and kicks sand on it. Disgusted with herself, she scoops it up, circles higher and higher, flapping her wide wings, gaining more and more height.

"No Sally. Put him back where you found him," Lizbeth scolds.

Sally flies out over the water, stares back at Lizbeth and drops the clam making a great splash.

Then, eyeing Lizbeth's backpack lying on the ground, Sally swoops down and pulls out a lined sheet of paper.

"My homework, Sally, that's my homework." Lizbeth watches the math problems that she had spent hours on last night float to the water.

"Oh no," Lizbeth could feel the tears begin. "Now I'll be late and won't have my math work." She plops herself down on a nearby rock.

Sally lands next to Lizbeth and offers her the wet soggy piece of paper hanging from her beak. She had rescued it from the waves. Up she flutters to Lizbeth's arm and coos that she's sorry.

"It's alright, I know you didn't mean it," Lizbeth pets Sally's head. "I better run to school – I'm already late," Lizbeth says as she carefully places the wet piece of paper into her bag and scampers down the road.

Lizbeth enters the school yard. It's empty. She had missed the morning bell.

"Oh my," she whispers, "Teacher and Mama will not be happy." She opens the door to Mrs. Riley's room and makes her way to her desk. The class becomes silent. Lizbeth has interrupted the first lesson for the third time this week.

Mrs. Riley stands at the blackboard, chalk in hand. She looks at Lizbeth and says, "Lizbeth, we will talk after school."

"Yes Ma'am."

Lizbeth passes in the soggy math paper when asked for her math homework. She sees Mrs. Riley's quizzical look.

"It was Sally," Lizbeth says.

Mrs. Riley nods and places it on the window sill to dry.

The final hour of the school day is spent learning geography, Lizbeth's favorite subject. She dreams of traveling the world. She sits with her Daddy and listens to his stories of people and places far away from

Windy Harbor.   When she grows up, she will see them all.

When it's time to pack up and leave for home, Mrs. Riley signals Lizbeth to wait and hands her a note saying, "Lizbeth, can you make a bigger effort next week to be on time?"

Lizbeth stuffs the note into her pocket and heads out the door, saying "Yes, Mrs. Riley, I'll try real hard. Sally had troubles this morning."

"I could see that, honey," Mrs. Riley tries not to smile. "You go right home."

Lizbeth doesn't hear Mrs. Riley's words because she's already singing her favorite song, *Over the Rainbow*. She twirls like Dorothy in the Wizard of Oz heading down her own yellow brick road leading to home. Maybe Mama will be so busy with Daddy's homecoming tomorrow that she won't be too disappointed that she was late to school again. Lizbeth crosses her fingers.

Tomorrow, she will visit Mr. James, the lighthouse keeper, to see if he is ready for Daddy's return. He knows everything about lighthouses. Last week, he showed her how the new generator works and how it will keep the lighthouse lit, even in a storm.

Lizbeth doesn't like storms. Betsy's father, a fisherman like her Daddy, had never returned to Windy Harbor after the last blizzard.

When Lizbeth asked Daddy what happened to Betsy's father, he hugged her and said, "Please don't worry about me, honey. I'll always find my way back to you and Mama. The lighthouse is my guardian and its light guides me home…."

2 FIONA

Lizbeth slips out from under her warm blankets to sit on her window seat.

"Fiona, are you out there?" she whispers, spotting only the twinkling stars in the dark Maine sky.

The ocean breeze blows the lace curtains around her. She peers into the darkness, but makes out only the sweep of the lighthouse's beacon across the black ocean.

Her mother had tucked her into bed, kissed her on the cheek and softly closed the bedroom door. As soon as Lizbeth heard her mother's footsteps on the stairs, she had popped out of bed, as she always did, and went to the window. She had to say goodnight to Fiona.

Maybe she's not coming tonight, Lizbeth thinks. But then, there, in the midst of the nighttime shadows, emerges a pinpoint of light above the rocks. It grows larger and larger until it arrives right in front of Lizbeth's nose.

Lizbeth giggles, "Fiona, I thought you forgot about me tonight."

Fiona, a firefly, blinks on and off twice, twirling around Lizbeth's head. This is her way of telling Lizbeth that she will never disappoint her - ever. She alights on Lizbeth's nose and kisses her goodnight as she had every night since Lizbeth was a tiny baby.

"Goodnight Fiona," Lizbeth yawns. "Remember, Daddy comes home tomorrow."

Fiona circles Lizbeth's head blinking on and off as fast as she can. She is very excited because she knows that Lizbeth's Daddy, a fisherman, has been gone a long time.

Lizbeth climbs into bed, snuggles under the blankets and falls asleep as the firefly lands on the window sill. Fiona closes her eyes and stays with Lizbeth till the first rays of sunshine appear at dawn. Then, seeing Lizbeth stir, Fiona stretches her wings and flies home past the craggy rocks.

3 MAMA

Lizbeth's eyes flutter open. She inhales the delightful smell of baking biscuits that wafts up from the kitchen. She stretches, slides out from under the covers, and pulls up her blankets, smoothing them like

Mama taught her. From the closet, she chooses her yellow flowered sundress, the one that Daddy loves best on her.

She throws open the bedroom door and runs barefoot down the stairs to where her mother stands cooking breakfast.

"Morning, sweetheart," Mama gives her a big hug. "You know what day it is?"

"Daddy's coming home," Lizbeth says, as she twirls around and around in the middle of the kitchen.

"Shhhh… calm down please. Yes, dear, tonight." Her mother leans in and holds Lizbeth's face in her two hands, "After you eat your breakfast, I want you to go out and play so I can do some work around the house. Would you do that for me?"

"Yes, Mama."

Lizbeth hops up on her chair, eats all of the biscuit and eggs on her plate, places her dish in the sink, and dances to the door.

"Don't forget your hat," Mama's words remind her.

Lizbeth jumps up and grabs her yellow sunbonnet from the hook, slips on her sandals and shuts the screen door behind her – without slamming it.

"Thank you, Lizbeth," her mother calls out after Lizbeth as she heads down the path toward the lighthouse.

4 FRIENDS

Lizbeth frolics and spins along the path to the lighthouse. It's a beautiful day – blue skies, white clouds and Daddy's coming home.

Out of the tall beach grass springs a fluffy grey rabbit. He lands right in front of Lizbeth's feet.

"Clarence, you scared me. I'm off to the lighthouse. Want to come?"

Clarence hops up and down swishing his fluffy white cotton tail as he bounds down the dirt path in front of Lizbeth.

Their next stop, the thicket, is the home of Rowena, the red fox. Lizbeth knocks on the gnarly thicket door, peeks in and calls out, "Wake up you sleepy head. Clarence and I are on our way to the lighthouse. Mama's cleaning the house for Daddy and she sent me off to play."

Rowena stretches, fluffs her long tail and yawns.

"Well, are you coming or not?" Lizbeth stands with her hands on her hips, her foot tapping as her mother did when she became impatient.

Rowena sticks her head out of the opening and notices that Clarence is sprinting up the hill toward the lighthouse. She squiggles out of the small door and dashes up the path after him, her tail curled over her head like a big red umbrella.

Lizbeth skips along the path behind her friends, until she spots the perfect daisy for her hat. As she bends down to pluck it, she hears a familiar buzz. It's Betty, the bumblebee, hard at work in a nearby buttercup.

"Betty, you are working too hard. Come join us at the lighthouse."

Betty gazes up at Lizbeth and then, soars into the air, buzzes

around her head, and lands on Lizbeth's bonnet rim, her dark almond

shaped eyes gazing down at Lizbeth.

"Come on, let's go, we're falling behind."

As the little parade proceeds to the lighthouse, Stuart, the squirrel,

appears beside Lizbeth. He chitter chatters away.

"No, Stuart, you know what happened the last time."

Stuart quiets and drops his head.

"Okay, you may come with us, but" Lizbeth says in a stern tone as

she wags her forefinger back and forth. "Not into the lighthouse.

Remember what happened last week?"

Stuart hangs his head again.

"Come along, but you can't eat Mr. James' newspaper. Promise?"

Stuart rears up on his hind legs and nods his head, his coal black eyes shining. Off he scampers to join Rowena, Clarence and Betty, his large fluffy tail puffed up behind him like a big grey and white billowing cloud.

5 THE STORM

The day passes with blue skies, white foaming clouds and the happy sounds of friends playing.   Mr. James waves to the group from the top of the lighthouse as he washes the lantern with his white cleaning rag. Even in the daytime, Mr. James keeps the light shining brightly.

And, Stuart, true to his word, doesn't enter the lighthouse and doesn't eat Mr. James' newspaper. All in all, it was a delicious kind of day… until it wasn't.

Lizbeth cheers on Clarence as he hops through the hopscotch squares drawn and numbered in the dirt.

"Clarence, where did your shadow go?" Lizbeth tosses her shell into the number five square.   She hops into the first square as Clarence

thumps a danger signal and points to the sky.   Standing on one leg, Lizbeth

looks up to where Clarence points and sees the sun hiding behind a big

black cloud.

"Oh my, it looks like a storm is coming, Clarence."   Lizbeth cups

her mouth and calls to her friends, "We better go – black storm clouds."

They hurry down the path toward home when a huge gust of wind

comes up behind Lizbeth and blows the yellow sunhat right off her

head.   The group stops and stares as she runs after it calling, "No, stop….

Come back."

Lizbeth climbs up on the rocks and watches it fly up, up, up.   As it

sails away, it looks like a splash of sunshine against the dark clouds building

over the water.

"Come back," she shouts and waves at it.   "Mama's going to be

angry."

Lizbeth's beautiful yellow straw hat turns into a tiny speck and then

disappears.   The black clouds march toward her.   The waves grow large and

crash on the rocks, spraying her with salt water.   She scurries away from the

edge, slips and slides on the wet rocks till she hits the ground with a

thud.   Her knee is scuffed and her dress is torn.   Mama won't be happy

when she returns home without her hat and wearing a ruined sundress.

"Oh no," she cries, rubbing at the dirt on her legs. She turns to Rowena, who waited at the bottom of the rocks for her, "How will Daddy find his way back? This storm feels big and his boat is small."

Rowena realizes what the dark clouds, the blowing winds, and the raging seas mean. She rubs her face against Lizbeth's leg telling her not to worry. Her Daddy had weathered storms like this before. He would bring his boat home safely.

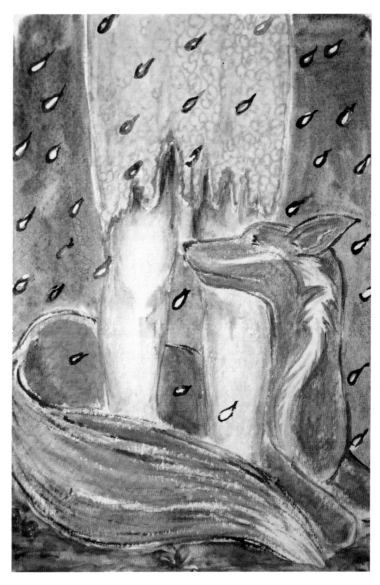

Big rain drops bounce off Lizbeth's head and cheeks. "Hurry," she yells to Rowena, as they scamper along the path, "everyone else is gone." Rowena ducks into her thicket and Lizbeth runs the rest of the way home.

6 THE LIGHTNING BOLT

That night at dinner, Mama speaks sternly to Lizbeth, "You know what I taught you, you are always to keep watch of the skies. If you had done that, you wouldn't have lost your hat or ruined your dress."

Lizbeth stares down at her steaming bowl of soup. Mama is correct, she hadn't been watchful. She had been having too much fun with her friends.

"Yes, Mama, I'm sorry. We were having so much fun and I wanted to win at hopscotch with Clarence."

"I'm sure you did honey, but isn't it a good thing that you and Clarence saw the storm coming when you did? A few more minutes and who knows what would have happened. But you need to be more alert to what's going on around you – storms come upon us quickly here. I want you to be safe."

Just as Mama finishes her sentence, the kitchen lights up when a huge flash of lightning strikes right outside their window. The house shakes as thunder rumbles across the water.

"See," Mama says as she watches the lightning flash, "It's a late summer thunderstorm and will pass quickly, like it came. But, while it's here, it's not safe to be outside."

Another bolt of lightning hits even closer and then, there is blackness.

"Lizbeth, you stay where you are. Do you hear me?" Mama stands and moves to the pantry. "Daddy keeps a lantern in the closet. I'll light it and we'll be fine."

Lizbeth disobeys her mother once again, slides off her chair and touches the walls till she reaches the door. "Mama, the lighthouse – it's black. The light is out. How will Daddy find his way home?"

"Lizbeth, didn't I ask you to stay put? What did we just finish talking about – your safety? You could hurt yourself in the dark," her mother speaks calmly as she reenters the kitchen with the lighted lantern. "Now, you remember, Mr. James bought a generator for the lighthouse. He showed you how it works, remember?"

"But it's not working."

"I'm sure it takes a few minutes to turn on. Please be patient, Lizbeth," her mother asks as she stands behind her. They watch the lightning illuminate the dark lighthouse from behind.

"See, the storm is going away. The waves and wind will die down

and Daddy will find his way home." Mama gently kisses the top of

Lizbeth's head.

"But where's the light? Daddy can't see where we are without the light. He'll crash on the rocks...," Lizbeth sobs.

"No he won't, honey, he'll be fine," her Mama pulls her close with a big hug, "I promise."

Lizbeth recalls Daddy's words, "The lighthouse is my guardian and its light guides me home." She fears that he won't be able to see where his fishing boat is headed without the sweeping light on top of the lighthouse. She has to fix the light. She throws open the door and darts down the path.

Her mother's voice echoes behind her, "Lizbeth, come back. It's too dark for you to be out there. Come back."

7 MR. JAMES

Lizbeth runs as fast as she can toward the lighthouse. She disobeyed her mother and knows that she will probably receive a big punishment. Nonetheless, she has to talk to Mr. James and find out why the generator didn't turn on the lantern light at the top of the lighthouse. When he demonstrated it, the large green metal box at the base of the lighthouse had hummed for a few minutes and then coughed and sputtered until it roared like a truck engine. Yet tonight it's silent as Lizbeth stands at the base of the lighthouse.

"Mr. James, Mr. James," she cries. Where is he?

Stuart emerges out of the darkness rubbing his eyes. Lizbeth's shouting woke him up. He trails her up the path, snapping his teeth louder and louder.

"Quiet Stuart, I have to find Mr. James. The light is out. See?" She points to the top of the lighthouse.

"Lizbeth, is that you?" a voice comes from the back of the

lighthouse. "Why are you out on such a stormy night?"

"Mr. James, I had to come. The light isn't on. Mama told me that the generator that you showed us would turn it on, but it didn't. What happened? How will my Daddy find us?"

Mr. James lets out a loud sigh as he sits on the top step. "Lizbeth, come and sit here with me for a minute."

Lizbeth looks at the wet step and then sits beside Mr. James. Her dress is already ruined.

Stuart climbs up each step and sits next to Lizbeth, ears turned to Mr. James waiting to hear his explanation.

"Well, it looks like lightning struck the generator."

"What does that mean?" Lizbeth says.

"It means that the lightning broke it and the light will not be on tonight. I'm sorry Lizbeth. It's nothing that I can fix."

"But you have to make it work. You have to," Lizbeth pleads. "If you don't, how will Daddy find his way home? He'll crash on the rocks, Mr. James, just like Betsy's father. You have to turn the light on for him." With that, Lizbeth begins to sob.

":I'm sorry, Lizbeth, truly I am. I wish there was something I could do. The lighthouse will be dark all night unless the electricity comes back on for everyone here on the peninsula."

.   "How do we turn the electricity back on?"

"We can't, sweetheart, the electric company has to come out

here and fix it. We just have to sit in the dark and wait."

"No, we have to make the lantern light."

Stuart chimes in with his squealing sounds.

"I think you should go back home. Your Mama must be worried sick about you being out here alone."

Lizbeth walks back down the path. "Stuart, what can we do?" she asks between hiccups. Lizbeth always gets the hiccups when she cries. "We can't just wait for days till the electricity comes back on. Daddy will be lost by then or will have crashed his boat. I have to do something, but what?"

8 STUART

Stuart doesn't answer Lizbeth right away; he seems to not to be listening to her as they continue along the path.

"Stuart, I don't want Daddy's boat to crash or be lost. I'd never see him again." She hiccups. "What can we do? We have to do something," she wipes the tears from her cheeks. "Do you think Mama's lantern would be enough to light the top of the lighthouse? Maybe Daddy could see that. I can run home...?"

Stuart stares up at Lizbeth. Then, he shakes his head "no."

"Let's gather all our friends together. One of them might come up with an idea – they might figure out what to do."

Then, as though he has a bright idea, Stuart dashes away, his squawks trailing behind him over the rocks.

"Stuart, come back. Where are you going? Our friends are this way," Lizbeth shouts as she follows the squirrel up to the top of the rocks.

"Stuart? Where are you?" Lizbeth stands alone in the

darkness. She hears nothing except the waves hitting the rocks below.

Dejected, she's about to return home when she spots Stuart running up over the rocks with a glow following behind him. The light becomes brighter and brighter.

Lizbeth stares. What is it? Then, she recognizes Fiona at the front of the streak of brilliance.

"Fiona, you've come." Lizbeth claps her hands in excitement. "Stuart, thank you so much. What a wonderful idea you had."

Stuart stands up chattering, so happy that he could help Lizbeth. She is his best friend.

Fiona buzzes around Lizbeth's head followed by all of her family. The string of lights that they create swirls around Lizbeth like a comet traveling through space.

Lizbeth races to the lighthouse followed by a trail of brilliant lights behind her, calling out, "Mr. James, Mr. James, open the door. The light is coming."

Mr. James throws open the door and, with a confused look on his face, ducks as the swarm of fireflies enters the lighthouse and swirls up the circular stairway. Up and up moves the brightness lighting each window it passes until the cloud of light reaches the lantern room.

"Lizbeth, where are you?"

Lizbeth hears her mother's voice come from the darkness behind her.

"Here, Mama."

"What did I tell you about being safe? I was worried sick about you being out here alone. You could trip and fall... I'd never find you."

"I'm sorry, Mama, I had to do something. Look." Lizbeth points to the brilliant light that swirls at the top of the lighthouse making the sky so bright that she could see the dark storm clouds moving away.

"Fiona and her family have given Daddy a guiding light."

"Oh honey, what a wonderful friend Fiona is. You are very lucky."

"Stuart did it. He found Fiona and she brought her family."

Mama hugs Lizbeth as they both look to the ocean.

"Do you think Daddy will be able to see Fiona and her family?" Lizbeth asks her mother.

"Oh, I'm sure. They shine as bright if not brighter than the lantern. Daddy will see them, I'm sure of it."

It is quiet with only the rhythmic slap of the waves hitting the rocks below breaking the silence of the night. Lizbeth and Mama stand silhouetted on the craggy rocks, holding each other's hand as they watch the dark ocean and wait for Daddy to arrive.

9 DADDY

"I don't see him yet, do you?" Lizbeth says.

"I don't honey, but he might have had to pull in somewhere because of the storm. He'll be along, I'm sure. Let's go home and wait there."

Then, almost at the same time that they turn to head down the path, there is the low rumble of a motor, a sound of a horn, and the flash of green and white lights – it's a fishing boat.

"It's Daddy," Lizbeth shouts, looking up at her Mama. "He sees Fiona and he's coming home." She breaks free of her mother and climbs to the highest point on the rocks. "Daddy, Daddy, we're here," she yells, waving her arms.

"Be careful Lizbeth. The rocks are still wet from the storm."

"I am, Mama," Lizbeth answers, hoping her Daddy can see her. Not sure, she climbs to the top flat rock and waves her arms high above her head.

And at that moment, Fiona, as though reading Lizbeth's thoughts leaves her family in the lighthouse and she flies down to shine her light on Lizbeth. She too wants Lizbeth's Daddy to see her.

"Oh look Fiona, it's Daddy."

"Thank you, Fiona. You and your wonderful family brought him home safely. I love you."

Fiona soars upward into the darkness. She twists and turns, making strange irregular movements that Lizbeth doesn't understand.

"Fiona, are you alright?" At that moment Lizbeth sees what Fiona has done.

Written across the sky is, "I love you too."

THE END

ABOUT THE AUTHOR

Judi Getch Brodman, a native of Massachusetts, received her Bachelor of Arts degree from Emmanuel College and her Masters of Science degree from Boston University. She studied creative writing at FAU. She is a professional artist, photographer and writer.

Early on, Judi was a software engineer and manager. She worked on space projects, airline reservation software, and radar systems, eventually becoming a well-known process improvement consultant. Throughout these years, she wrote technical articles, newsletters, and process books. She spoke at conferences worldwide, even worked in the Marshall Islands.

Eventually, the urge to write creatively became too strong and she left her technical profession and began a new chapter of her life – writer and artist.

Judi has published a two part travel story on Ireland, The Many Faces of Ireland, and a fictional short story, Safe Harbor. She has also written a cozy mystery, She's Not You, hopefully soon to be published and a historical love/time travel novel, The Sea Captain's Women still in editing. She has two other novels in the works.

Fiona – the Lighthouse Firefly is her first children's book. Will it be her last? We just have to wait and see.

53587605R00028